THE EMPEROR'S NEW CLOTHES

by
HANS CHRISTIAN ANDERSEN

Retold and Illustrated by
NADINE BERNARD WESTCOTT

An Atlantic Monthly Press Book
Little, Brown and Company
BOSTON   TORONTO

Based on *Andersen's Tales for Children*
(published in 1861 by D. Appleton and Co., New York)

Library of Congress Cataloging in Publication Data

Andersen, H. C. (Hans Christian), 1805–1875
    The emperor's new clothes.

    Translation of: Kejserens nye klæder.
    "An Atlantic Monthly Press book."
    Summary: During a royal procession, an emperor
wears an invisible suit of clothes made for him by
two swindlers.
    [1. Fairy tales]   I. Westcott, Nadine Bernard, ill.
II. Title.
PZ8.A542Em 1984   [E]   83-19610
ISBN 0-316-93123-3
ISBN 0-316-93124-1 (pbk.)

For Becky, Wendy, Christine,

Jenn, Katie, and Dana

There once lived an emperor who was very fond of new clothes. While other kings might like to parade their soldiers or spend an evening at the theater, there was nothing

this emperor loved more than trying on new clothes —
which his servants would bring him in great stacks, morning, noon, and night.

Other servants toiled endlessly to keep the emperor's vast wardrobe cleaned and pressed. The kingdom's most learned scholars were kept constantly on hand to advise him on his choice of clothing. Any outfit the emperor might desire must be ready for him at a moment's notice.

7

The emperor had a different outfit for every hour of the day, and clothes for each day of the week.

CLOTHES TO PLAY IN ↓

CLOTHES TO LOOK HANDSOME IN ↓

CLOTHES T

For no matter how great or small the occasion, he wanted to wear just the right clothes to make his subjects see him as a wise and able ruler.

CLOTHES TO LOOK BRAVE IN ↓

CLOTHES TO LOOK SMART IN ↓

K SUPER IN ↓

9

But his outfits never seemed quite right.

10

And his clothes were apt to turn up in the most inconvenient places.

11

Not even his wife or his most trusted ministers could persuade him that he need not worry so much about his royal attire.

13

One day, two swindlers traveled to the castle, pretending to be weavers.

"We can weave the most beautiful cloth imaginable!" the first told the emperor. "And, what is more, the clothes made from our fabrics are invisible to anyone who is either foolish or unfit for his office."

"Not everyone, of course, is able to wear such finery," added the second. "But they are obviously the perfect clothes for a wise ruler like yourself!"

The emperor thought of how wisely he could rule his people if only he had such an outfit. "Why, not only would I look grand, but with those clothes on, I could find out which of my ministers is unfit for his post; I could tell the wise from the foolish. This cloth must be woven for me at once!"

The weavers set up their looms and worked late into the night.

No one was allowed to see their work, until...

17

the emperor sent his wisest and most
trusted minister to see what had been made.

The weavers begged the minister to step closer. They named all the colors, and described the pattern in great detail. The minister paid close attention to all they said, for, unable to believe his own eyes, he wanted to be able to repeat it exactly to the emperor.

The minister hurried back and described the new clothes to the emperor, exactly as they had been described to him.

"Why, you must wear them tomorrow in the royal procession!" the emperor's wife cried. "It is the perfect chance to show all of your subjects what a wise and magnificent ruler you are."

The next morning the weavers at last announced, "The clothes are finished!" They brought in the royal robes and dressed the emperor in them, taking great care to see that there were no loose threads and that the royal garments hung just right. The emperor could scarcely believe his eyes, but he kept quiet as a mouse, lest his subjects think him a fool.

People had come from every corner of the kingdom to see the magnificent new clothes.

24

As the emperor set forth in the royal procession, the crowd grew silent. *My new clothes must be so stunning, no one can find the right words to praise them!* thought the emperor. He lifted his head and marched on proudly, until...

25

a small child's voice could be heard clearly to say, "But he has no clothes on!"

"He has no clothes on!" the people echoed, each feeling secretly foolish not to have spoken up earlier.

What could the emperor possibly do now?

Without any of his royal outfits to help him look intelligent or brave, the emperor realized it was more important now than ever to act like a king. He lifted his head even higher, and stood even taller, and continued the procession. Never had he felt so foolish . . . but never had he acted so wisely.

Seeing their ruler's extraordinary courage, the crowd began to cheer, more loudly than the emperor had ever heard them.

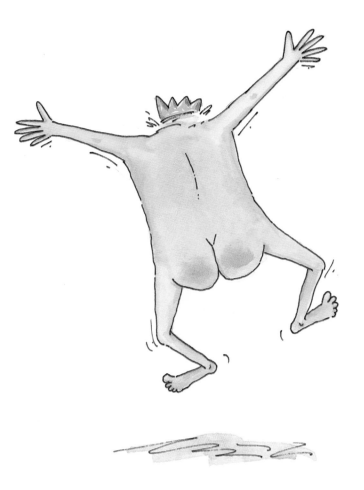

"Long live the king!"

THE EMPEROR'S WARDROBE

You can create new clothes for the emperor. Use these drawings as models to make your own paper doll and clothes. Trace them carefully on a separate sheet of paper; color, and cut out. And don't stop there — how many other outfits can you design for him?